Taking Care of Myself

Getting Exercise

By Meg Gaertner

level 2
little blue readers

www.littlebluehousebooks.com

Little Blue House is distributed by North Star Editions:
sales@northstareditions.com | 888-417-0195

Produced for Little Blue House by Red Line Editorial.

Photographs ©: Shutterstock Images, cover, 9, 10, 13 (top), 13 (bottom), 16, 24 (top left), 24 (top right), 24 (bottom right); iStockphoto, 4, 7, 15 (top), 15 (bottom), 19, 21, 23, 24 (bottom left)

Library of Congress Control Number: 2021916793

ISBN
978-1-64619-491-9 (hardcover)
978-1-64619-518-3 (paperback)
978-1-64619-569-5 (ebook pdf)
978-1-64619-545-9 (hosted ebook)

Printed in the United States of America
Mankato, MN
012022

About the Author

Meg Gaertner enjoys reading, writing, dancing, and being outside. She lives in Minnesota.

Table of Contents

Getting Exercise

Exercise keeps the body healthy and strong. A healthy body lets you do the things you enjoy.

Exercise can also make you feel better.
It can help you sleep better, too.

Try to exercise every day. There are many fun activities to choose from.

PETZL

basketball

Sports

Playing a sport such as basketball is exercise. Players practice and play often.

You can skate in hockey.

You can run in soccer.

hockey

soccer

You can punch in boxing.

You can kick in karate.

boxing

karate

running

Keep Moving

Walking or running
is exercise.
Swimming is exercise, too.

Playing tag is exercise. Riding a bike is exercise, too.

bike

Maybe you like dancing the most.

There are many fun ways to get exercise!

dancing

Daily exercise leads to a strong, healthy body. A strong, healthy body leads to a happier life.

Glossary

basketball

hockey

boxing

soccer

Index